Mighty Minds

Mighty Minds

L J Whelan

Matador
9 Priory Business Park,
Wistow Road, Kibworth Beauchamp,
Leicestershire. LE8 0RX
Tel: 0116 279 2299
Email: books@troubador.co.uk
Web: www.troubador.co.uk/matador
Twitter: @matadorbooks

ISBN 978 1788033 404

British Library Cataloguing in Publication Data.
A catalogue record for this book is available from the British Library.

Printed and bound by CPI Group (UK) Ltd, Croydon, CR0 4YY
Typeset in 13pt Adobe Garamond Pro by Troubador Publishing Ltd, Leicester, UK

Matador is an imprint of Troubador Publishing Ltd

This book is dedicated to

Rhys Devereaux – my inspiration

Go for the things that you want to achieve
Never give up and always believe.

THANK YOU to my MAGNIFICENT team...

The Swellies Cafe, *the Pitch* – where the *Mighty Minds* were created. What can I say?... the grooviest, hippest, coolest café in North Wales. Liam recommends the cheese sandwich – the BESTEST cheese sandwich he has ever tasted. A special thank you to Eddie for his constant support and AMAZING food.

Spencer Hall, my *manager* at Auria Management – who enables every team to win the trophy. Thank you for breathing and believing.

Natalie Adams, my *illustrator – a fantastic striker* who brought the magic of *Mighty Minds* so beautifully to life. Thank you.

Charlie Gardner, my *editor – a skilful striker* who turned words into magic. Thank you my friend.

Hayden Jones, my *coach* – the silent champion – for flying high in the sky with me on this one. Thank you for the inspirational conversations.

Mike White & Jamie, my *referees* – for blowing the whistle every time I went offside. Those ginger teas and wise words were crucial.

Phil Whelan, my *dynamic defender* – thank you for always defending my corner.

Dan Parry, website designer – a *masterful midfielder* – thank you for the digital creations.

Dave Smith, my *goalie* – a great save. Thank you.

Scott Griffith, military aviation consultant – a *perfect striker* who cannot be matched for his precision. Thank you for the conversations and education.

Sean Wheelan, *my substitute* – for joining the game in the final moments ensuring the ultimate victory.

Betty and John Devereaux, *the world's greatest supporters* – thank you for your constant support and belief. Thank you for everything.

Hratch Ogali, the world's greatest – *my own personal coach* who set me on the path to my destiny. A blessing.

Seto Ogali, *a creative midfielder* – thank you for keeping me flying in the world of my imagination. Let's fly!

Isabella Jones, *keeper of my spiritual home* at Hotel Port Dinorwic – thank you for your constant support, belief and guidance.

Liam, Lucia, Harry and Holly, *my inspiration* – thank you for being the bestest, the cutest and the cleverest. Never stop believing!

MOST IMPORTANTLY – THANK YOU TO ALL OF YOU AWESOME AND AMAZING BOYS AND GIRLS FOR READING THE MIGHTY MINDS BOOK – YOU ARE THE WORLD'S GREATEST.

CHAPTER 1

Dream the Magic!

Liam pulled on his pyjama bottoms. He didn't like evenings very much as he always had to go to bed early. And he especially didn't like Friday evenings as he had football the next day and was always way too excited to sleep. Liam loved football more than anything else in the world. The next best thing in the world was his dog, Jack.

"Liam, are you in bed yet?" his dad shouted from the hallway.

"Yes!" Liam hurried, pulling his top over his head and leapt into bed. "Dad, can you tell me a story?"

"No story tonight, Liam," said Dad, switching the bedroom light off. "Good night, Son."

Liam pulled the covers up over his head. He couldn't stop thinking about the match tomorrow.

He knew that his team had to win to be in the semi-finals, but he had been playing rubbish in the last few games.

He tossed and turned, scrunching his eyes closed, forcing himself to go to sleep. Harry, his best friend, told him his granddad taught him to count sheep to help him sleep. Harry said it always worked for him, so Liam thought he would give it a try.

He tried to picture a sheep in his mind, but all he could see were baby lambs – little white lambs running towards a white fence. He could see something on their feet… boots, little black and white football boots!

Liam chuckled to himself.

The first lamb jumped the fence.

Then the second and then the third – all wearing their football boots.

As they landed they began to take their positions in the field.

As if by magic, a ball bounced onto the grass.

The lambs began to run, dribbling the ball with their noses – just like Liam's dog, Jack. Liam got annoyed with Jack whenever he did this, but he also found it very funny.

The lamb playing centre forward (Liam's position) ran and ran. He ran so fast the other sheep couldn't keep up with him. He was more like a dog than a lamb.

He dribbled, he dodged, he turned, and he weaved. His head bowed low as he tossed the ball up into the air, and watched it fly into the back of the net.

Dad opened the bedroom door and poked his head
in.

Liam was sleeping deeply and dreaming. "I
wish that we could win the tournament and score
hundreds of goals," his face seemed to say…

It was the morning of the semi-finals and Liam's team were running onto the pitch past *The World's Greatest* – the statue that stands at his training ground. The statue of the world's greatest footballer standing tall with his boot on a football – the football that Coach Hall makes his team touch for good luck before every game.

Liam was always a little scared of the statue. It was very big, and it was the greatest footballer in the world. And that was all that Liam had ever wanted to be…

Liam knew he had a lot of hard work to do to lift the cup at Wembley, so he decided to see if he could get some extra good luck from *The World's Greatest*.

Liam placed both hands on the football, closed his eyes and made the biggest wish he had ever wished.

It was bigger than the sky…

It was bigger than the sea…

It was bigger than his baby sister's poo!

He wished, and he wished, and he wished, and he WISHED!

Suddenly, the ball became hotter and hotter, then redder and redder, then brighter and brighter, until it was a ball of dazzling, white light!

"Good morning, Liam…"

Liam leapt away, his hands were as hot as his favourite hot-and-spicy pizza.

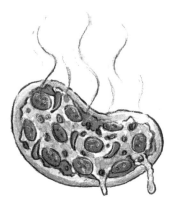

He rubbed his eyes and ears. Where did that voice come from?

"Liam, do you want your team to win the cup?"

Liam stood staring at the flashing ball.

"Liam, I asked you a question."

Liam froze. The voice was deep and powerful but it was also very kind and slow. It reminded Liam of his sister's talking teddy, Samuel. Samuel was cute and funny but sometimes loud and scary – especially when his baby sister, Lucia, played with him over and over again.

Liam nodded.

"I can't hear you," the football flashed.

"Yes!" Liam replied.

"OK Liam," said the ball. "Now listen very carefully. If you really want to win the cup, you *can* win the cup – but you have to promise me you will do exactly as I say. If you do that, your team will be the greatest!"

Liam didn't feel scared anymore. He had that same feeling in his tummy that he got on Christmas Eve when he went to bed; that excited feeling that Father Christmas was going to come in the morning with lots of presents.

"I have great power, and I am going to take you and your team on a very special journey. To speak to me you have to close your eyes, tap me three times and wish as hard as you can. Do you think you can do that, Liam?"

"Liam…"

"Liam, Liam… It's time to get up…" his mum's voice whispered in his ear. "Wake up, Liam!" His mum kissed him on the forehead – something his mum did every morning, and something that Liam disliked. He was a boy not a girl.

Liam opened his eyes and leapt out of bed.

"I have never seen you get out of bed that quickly!" said Mum, astonished.

But Liam didn't have time to speak to his mum; he wanted to get to the pitch to tell Harry, his best friend, all about his dream.

Liam's dad was at the door with the car keys in his hand. Liam's dad always took him to football.

"Dad, our team has special powers!" Liam burbled.

"The only way you are going to have special powers, my son, is by practice!" his dad retorted.

Liam slung his boots over his shoulder and ran out the door.

"Liam, have you brushed your hair?" called Mum.

But Liam didn't look back. He ran towards the car, dragging his bag and coat along the floor behind him. "Pick up your coat, Liam!" his mum's voice trailed behind him.

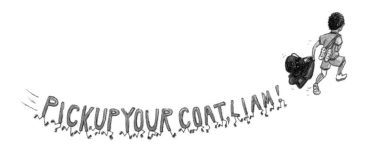

PICK UP YOUR COAT, LIAM!

Unable to contain his excitement, Liam jumped into the car.

"Now, Son, they are going to be a tough team to beat today. Do you remember what I told you?"

Liam nodded.

"So what is our motto?" Dad said expectantly, waiting for the answer.

"No one remembers second place…" Liam replied quietly.

"Good boy!" Dad smiled, tapping Liam on the head.

"We should have brought Jack along," Liam giggled.

"He would chase the ball and eat it, and there would be no game!" laughed Dad.

Liam thought about his dog chewing the ball and chuckled. Jack always chewed his footballs!

CHAPTER 2

The Higher Pitch

Dad's car turned into a large driveway, which led to a huge football pitch.

WORLDS GREATEST

Liam leapt out of the car and ran towards the clubhouse. He couldn't wait to tell Harry, his best friend, all about his dream. He ran into the changing room and found Harry getting his kit – his perfect kit that his mum always made sure was neat and tidy – out of his bag. And while Harry carefully laid out his shirt and shorts, Liam started to whisper in his ear…

"Harry, come on. We can't be late!" Liam tugged on Harry's shirt. Harry rushed to tie his football boots.

As quick as lightning, the boys ran through the changing room, onto the field, then skidded to a halt.

"Now, Harry, watch the ball!" Liam instructed.

Liam looked up at *The World's Greatest* and placed his hands on the football. He closed his eyes, made a really big, strong wish, and waited… but nothing happened.

"Guess it was just a silly dream," Harry giggled.

"I'm sure it will work," said Liam. "The football lit up in my dream… It was magic, Harry, and if I do this we will be the greatest team!"

Harry stood next to him, waiting. Liam put his hands on the ball again and wished the biggest wish he had *ever* wished. He wished with all of his heart. And that was when he remembered he had to close his eyes, and tap the ball three times, otherwise it wouldn't work.

So he tapped once… the ball became hotter and hotter.

He tapped twice… the ball became redder and redder.

He tapped three times… the ball became brighter and brighter. It was the brightest white light that he had ever seen.

There was a loud rumble, as loud as a lion's roar; the ground began to shake and the wind blew so strong they could barely stand. The earth heaved and growled until the pitch began to move, and Liam and Harry moved with it… up and up and up, faster and faster. Liam and Harry held each other tightly, but they could barely see each other's faces in the dazzling light from the surface below. Up and up, faster and faster, then… stop! The light faded… The wind dropped… and Liam and Harry found themselves standing on a goal line… a goal line in the clouds with nothing beneath them. Their football pitch had disappeared.

Somewhere, far below Liam and Harry, the ground rumbled and shook once more, before it screamed and wailed with a high-pitch echo that made them cover their ears. Something was coming… and it was coming through the clouds.

Was it a dinosaur?

Was it Tiger Spirit?

The CUTEST, CHATTIEST,

FASTEST, FUNNIEST,
SUNNIEST,
SPEEDIEST,

SUPEREST CAR you will
ever meet.

Could it be Hawk the hunter?

The

HUNGRIEST,

HANDSOMEST,

FIERCEST,

FEARSOMEST,

AWESOMEST FIGHTER JET you will ever meet.

Liam and Harry stood frozen. Before their eyes appeared the most magical, magnificent thing they had ever seen in their lives.

It was BIGGER than a dinosaur.

It was BETTER than Liam's most favourite hot and spicy pizza, BIGGER than his baby sister's poo and LARGER than the sky and the sea.

It was even bigger and better than a giant Easter Egg.

They watched as the BIGGEST, BRIGHTEST and BEST football pitch in the world rose high above them.

CHAPTER 3

Breathe...
The Power of a Tiger...
The Strength of a Bear

"Good morning, Liam and Harry!" boomed *The World's Greatest*. "Welcome to my world! It is time to begin your journey to becoming the best footballers that you can be…"

Liam and Harry looked up. It felt as if the voice was coming from the top of the never-ending spiral stairs above them.

"What are you waiting for? Go, follow your dream!" *The World's Greatest* encouraged them.

Liam and Harry ran as fast as they could up the stairs – the steps were steep and seemed to go on for ever. As they reached the top they were greeted by a blinding white light, but this time it came from the biggest, brightest floodlights lighting up the biggest, lushest, greenest football pitch.

The grass was the perfect length, and the lines bright white; it looked as if no one had ever played football here before.

Liam and Harry stepped out onto the pitch. A loud bell chimed over the loudspeakers, and, as the floodlights dimmed, an electronic sign lit up in red above the goal with the word "BELIEVE".

"Believe!" boomed *The World's Greatest*. "That's your key word. We are going to create a system… our belief system," he continued. "You are going to learn to be the best… and being the best begins with the breath!"

Confused, Liam and Harry stayed silent.

"Do you know the meaning of your names?" asked the *World's Greatest*.

Liam and Harry were unsure.

"Liam, you are a warrior! And, Harry, you are a ruler! Remember that and we will come back to it when we train with your team."

Liam and Harry glanced at each other, secretly smirking.

"Now I want you to both take a deep breath in and shout out the words 'Power of a tiger – strength of a bear!'"

Liam and Harry began to giggle. They felt very embarrassed.

"What is wrong?" asked *The World's Greatest*.

Liam plucked up all of his courage to answer. "It's a bit… well… silly…"

A loud laugh echoed around the stadium.

"Now that is silly!" said *The World's Greatest*. "You obviously don't want to be the greatest…"

Liam and Harry looked at each other as they shouted together, "Yes we do! Yes we do!"

"Well if you want to be the greatest then you are going to have to be silly sometimes, because that's what champions do – they go beyond what is possible."

Liam and Harry looked puzzled. They wanted to be the greatest footballers more than anything in the world.

"Now if I say something, I want you to do it the very first time I ask you. Is that understood?"

Liam and Harry smiled at each other, took in the deepest breaths they could and shouted, "Power of a tiger! Strength of a bear!"

"Fantastic!!! Oh, I'm really scared! I'm shaking... not!" *The World's Greatest* joked.

Liam and Harry burst out laughing.

"Try it again. I want you to do five more..."

The boys took in an even deeper breath and shouted as loud as they could, "Power of a tiger! Strength of bear!"

"Is that the best you can do?" *The World's Greatest* laughed. "Louder! I can't hear you. I want to see the power of that tiger and the strength of that bear!"

The boys took even deeper breaths and shouted even louder.

"POWER OF A TIGER!"

"STRENGTH OF A BEAR!"

"POWER OF A TIGER!"

"STRENGTH OF A BEAR!"

"Hmmmn… Not bad…" said *The World's Greatest*. "Now I want you to take the deepest breaths in through your noses until there is no air left, and then I am going to count to five, and you are going to blow out through your mouths until I stop counting… Are you ready?"

The boys nodded in readiness.

"Are you sure you can do this?"

The boys smiled and nodded.

"Are you sure you want to be the greatest footballers in the world?"

The boys nodded crazily.

"I can't hear you…'

"Yes! Yes!" the boys shouted.

"OK, here we go! 1, 2, 3…"

The boys took in the deepest breaths they could and clenched their fists, pushing down to give them more power.

"4... 5!"

The World's Greatest's voice echoed through the stadium as Liam and Harry began breathing out.

"Now what do you have?"

Liam and Harry shouted louder than ever.

"THE POWER OF A TIGER!"

"THE STRENGTH OF A BEAR!"

Harry and Liam couldn't believe how loud they sounded. They even scared themselves.

"That was like the loudest ever!" Liam exclaimed.

"Fantastic! That was fantastic!" *The World's Greatest* was very pleased with Liam and Harry. "I think you both deserve to go on a little adventure for working so hard. So now I want you to close your eyes and hold hands…"

Liam and Harry looked at each other unable to contain their excitement as they grasped each other's hands.

"Are you ready?"

The boys nodded.

"Are you *sure* you are ready?" *The World's Greatest* joked.

The boys were serious.

"Are you sure you want to be the greatest footballers in the world?"

The boys nodded impatiently.

"I can't hear the tiger and the bear?"

"Yes! Yes!" Liam and Harry shouted out.

Their voices echoed throughout the stadium as the ground beneath them began to shake, and the wind blew so strong they could barely stand. And as the ground shook the pitch began to move… again…

CHAPTER 4

Believe it is the Best Football in the World

Liam and Harry looked down as the football pitch began to change from lush, green grass to dry, dusty and sandy mud.

Liam watched as his football kit vanished and was replaced by plain white shorts and a plain white T-shirt.

"It's not the kit that makes the player, it is his belief!" *The Worlds Greatest*'s voice was stronger and louder this time.

The lights faded and the goalposts began to shrink until they were tiny – so tiny, Liam thought to himself, that the ball might not even fit into the goals. Not even the baby lambs from his dream would fit into them.

Then Liam saw two balls in the middle of the pitch. Dust flew up as the boys ran across the surface – the balls looked a little odd and differently sized, but Liam and Harry couldn't wait to get to them.

Liam picked up the small ball. "This isn't a ball, it's a pair of socks!"

"This isn't a ball, it's a grapefruit!" shouted Harry, picking up the larger "football".

The both looked at each other, confused.

"If you believe they are a grapefruit and a pair of socks, then that is all they will ever be!" explained *The World's Greatest*. "However, if you believe they are the *best footballs in the world*, as you did when you first saw them, then they will be the best balls in the world!"

Liam and Harry giggled.

"Now, I want you to believe each ball is the best ball in the world, made for the best footballer in the world."

The boys giggled harder.

"The ball is your friend; it is there for you to help you to win. Do not focus on the goal. Focus on the ball!" continued *The World's Greatest*. "For our first lesson, I want you to play opposite each other, and I want you to see how many goals you can score."

Liam and Harry looked confused.

"But how can we play against each other when we have no one to pass the ball to?" Liam asked.

"You will take the ball, then run as fast as you can to the goal and score!"

"The goal is tiny," Harry observed.

"Yes, but the balls are tiny so you won't have a problem. It will be easy."

Liam and Harry stood either side of the socks trying not to laugh.

"Now remember, these are the best footballs in the world, made for the best football players. You are both the greatest!"

"We can't both be the greatest!" Liam retorted.

"Who says you can't both be the greatest?"

"We can't both win…"

"Who says you can't both win?"

"There's only one winner," Harry reasoned.

"The best footballers in the world know that if the team wins the game then everyone is a winner. Believe you are the greatest and you will be the greatest that you can be!"

"My dad said winning is about practice!" Harry shouted boldly.

"Your dad is right. Practice is what Coach Hall will teach you. I will teach you how to listen, to be aware and to trust. I will teach you the secret of football. With me you will learn the love and magic of the game. The Belief System is the magical key to becoming the greatest. As soon as the whistle blows you will be the best footballer on the pitch."

Liam was troubled. He didn't like the idea of playing against Harry – he liked passing to Harry and playing *with* him.

"If you want to be the best, you have to challenge what is comfortable." The football of *The World's Greatest* flashed as he spoke. "You will feel uncomfortable against each other, but if you can do this you can take on anyone. Now score that goal. I want goals from both of you!"

CHAPTER 5

FUN – Free Uninhibited and Natural

"Now for some fun – it's time for the FUN Bubble!" *The World's Greatest* said, but without a trace of fun in his voice. Liam thought he sounded a little bit like his dad but not as angry.

"Do you know what FUN stands for?"

"Football!" Liam shouted.

"Computer games!" yelled Harry.

"No school!" added Liam.

"No homework," Harry continued.

Liam and Harry couldn't stop laughing. *The World's Greatest* laughed, too, and then he became very serious indeed.

"FUN stands for… Free, Uninhibited and Natural!"

Liam and Harry didn't really understand what he meant.

"Don't worry about understanding the meaning right now, you will understand in time. For now, you are going to just feel it… Be free, be uninhibited and it will all come naturally in this environment."

The World's Greatest paused to let the message sink in.

"Now let me see how many goals you can score!" he exclaimed, and blew his referee's whistle.

Harry took the first kick: the socks trickled in front of him, barely moving. He kicked them harder but they were difficult to control. He realised he had to take it slower, to think, but then Liam tackled him, stepping on the socks and flattening them. Liam kicked again, but the socks hardly moved. He knew that Harry was a faster runner than him, so how would he ever dribble with the socks and beat Harry to the goal?

"Do not think about being fast, Liam. Imagine you are an eagle and you are flying down the pitch… Stretch out your arms and fly!" *The World's Greatest*'s voice echoed over the loudspeaker.

Liam pushed faster and harder, stumbling over the socks.

"Put your arms out, Liam. I said fly!"

"It's silly, you don't fly in football!" Liam shouted back.

"All the greatest footballers in the world fly – they just don't let you see it. When you are here you do as I say. Now, fly like an eagle!"

Liam put his arms out to the side like an eagle. He felt very silly, and as he looked over his shoulder he could see Harry catching up with him.

"Liam, fly to those socks – those socks are your friends, they will do what you want them to. It is just you and the socks – swoop down on them and flip them into the back of that net!"

Liam ran faster, his arms out to the side. For a moment, he felt like he was an eagle flying high in the sky and looking down on the tiny socks on the pitch. The socks looked minute now, making it easy for him to swoop down and flip them into the back of the net. He imagined himself swooping; the ball was coming closer; but Harry was even closer behind him – he was almost at the ball too!

Liam spread his wings; his feet ran faster than they had ever run before; he felt as though they weren't touching the ground; he felt like he was flying.

"Power of a tiger, strength of a bear. Take that breath and fly through the air!" *The World's Greatest* shouted out.

Liam lifted his foot and lobbed the ball into the net. "Woo-hoooo!!! Yeah! Yeah, I scored!" Liam celebrated. "Power of a tiger, strength of a bear. Yeah, yeah, yeah! Yeah, yeah, YEAH!!!"

Liam jumped up and down. He had scored with the smallest socks in the smallest football net in the world. Harry turned away, kicking the dirt. Liam ran behind him.

"Harry, I scored. Did you see that? I have never scored like that before!"

Harry nodded.

"Harry, what's wrong?" *The World's Greatest* asked.

Harry didn't answer.

"Harry, if I ask you a question you must answer me."

"I'm angry because I didn't get the ball," Harry replied.

"The ball is gone, you can't get it now; it's in the

past. Now is all that matters. It is your turn; just focus on what is in front of you. Focus on the ball – the ball that is your friend – and on scoring that goal."

Harry kicked the ground again and got into position. The whistle blew. Harry kicked the grapefruit and went after it. Faster than he expected, Liam ran up the pitch and tackled Harry. They twisted and turned until the grapefruit ran free and trickled into touch. Harry stopped.

"There are no lines here, Harry," *The World's Greatest* explained. "There are no rules on the higher pitch, just keep playing. You are free to kick and run. This is playing just for FUN!"

Harry dragged the grapefruit back with his boot and set off down the edge of the half.

"Look to the pitch, aim for the ball. In front of the crowd you have it all!"

The World's Greatest shouted encouragingly.

Harry could see the goal but he had no one to pass to. Liam was to the left of him, looking to make another tackle; he would normally pass to Liam, but he couldn't. Instead he turned, flipped the ball over Liam's head and watched as the grapefruit rolled free towards the goal.

"Harry, I want you to imagine you are a cheetah; the fastest cheetah – nothing can catch you. The only thing you want in the world is the ball in the net; and there is nothing that can stop you because you are the fastest creature on the planet!"

Harry was determined to get the ball in the net. He ran faster than he had ever run before. He ran like a cheetah leaving Liam lost in a trail of dust.

"Power of a tiger, strength of a bear. Take that breath and fly through the air!" *The World's Greatest* shouted out...

Liam watched as Harry smashed the grapefruit into the back of the net.

"Yes, yes, YES! I scored!" Harry ran over to Liam as they celebrated together.

CHAPTER 6

You are the Greatest!

"Now for the best exercise of all," *The World's Greatest* announced. "Liam, I want you to go to the other end of the pitch – I want you to run from one goal all the way down to the other. And Harry, you are going to cheer and shout, 'Liam is the greatest' as he runs. OK?"

Harry nodded awkwardly.

"And Liam," *The World's Greatest* continued, "you are going to shout 'I am an eagle and I am the greatest!' as you run. OK?"

Both boys felt a little bit shy and silly.

The whistle sounded and Liam ran as fast as he could towards the other goal. Harry and *The World's Greatest* cheered him all the way.

He was half way down the pitch when he heard the voice in his head again, "Fly like an eagle!" He turned his attention to the goal – there was nothing but him, the goal and the sound of the cheering from Harry, his best friend, and the greatest footballer to have ever lived. He put his arms out like an eagle and flew like lightning to the goal.

He thought to himself that this had been the most fun he had ever had – today, he had been the winner.

"Now, Liam, it's your turn to cheer Harry…"

Liam ran speedily to the touchline as Harry set off.

"Harry is the greatest!" Liam shouted at the top of his voice as *The World's Greatest* joined in.

"Run like a cheetah!" Harry focused on the goal, the goal that felt like his friend today. There was nothing but him and the sound of cheering from the greatest footballer to have ever lived and Liam, his best friend.

Harry ran faster than a cheetah. The smile on his face was like the smile that he had on his birthday – today felt like his birthday! Today was fun, and today he was a winner.

"I am so proud of you both for listening and doing what I asked of you. That is the way champions are made: by listening and doing," *The World's Greatest* praised them. "Today, you have learned the first steps in the Belief System – the first two tools to becoming the greatest: 'Breathe and Believe!'"

Liam felt proud of himself. He wished his dad could have been there to see him. Today he and Harry were one step closer to being the best footballers that they could be.

"I want you to do the Tiger and Bear exercise for me every day until I see you next," *The World's World's Greatest* explained. "It is the most important thing to becoming, and staying, the greatest. It is how I became the greatest footballer in the world...

"Football is simple. It's about giving and receiving; controlling the ball and being ready to accept the pass to you. It's that simple. And when you have the power of a tiger and the strength of a bear on top of that, you can do anything. Stay strong! Stay happy!"

Liam and Harry looked at each other. They both knew it was a bit silly, but they wanted to be the best footballers that they could be; so they promised *The World's Greatest* that they would do the Tiger and Bear exercise every day.

"This was just the first lesson in the magic of the most beautiful game on Earth," mused *The World's Greatest*. "We have many adventures to go on as a team, but that... is for another day..."

"Do you mean that we can bring our team here to meet you?" Liam asked boldly.

"Of course – I want to meet the whole team. To

be the world's greatest team you need to train as a team. The only way you can win is as a team, and I will make you the best Mighty Minds, little-league team that you can be!"

CHAPTER 7

Love of the Game

All of a sudden, the boys felt themselves dropping, faster and faster, their arms above their heads, as they flew through the air. There was a loud bump as Liam and Harry landed on their training pitch.

The boys sat up in the centre of the pitch, both of them now dressed in their normal training kit.

"Liam… Harry… what are you doing?" Coach Hall shouts from the line. "Stop day dreaming and get up off the floor!"

Liam and Harry ran over as the whole team gathered around their manager.

"Now, Team, what do we do before every game?"

Liam and Harry watched their team-mates line up in front of *The World's Greatest*. They couldn't wait to share his secret – his secret of how this team could become the best. They watched as each of their friends ran past *The World's Greatest*, touching his football as they went.

First to touch the ball was Chin – a midfielder who was always the first to the ball in the game, but Coach Hall was always telling him to think less and do more.

Next up was, Ollie – a strong and powerful defender, but Coach Hall was always telling him to stand up straight and to stop looking at the floor.

Annabel bounded along. She was quite small for a goalie but she could leap very high. Coach Hall always said she talked and jumped around far too much.

Dominic the dynamic defender drifted past. Coach Hall was always telling him to listen more.

Yusef played in defence, too. Coach Hall was always telling him to stop dreaming and get real.

Then it was Harry's turn. Harry had been Liam's best friend since primary school, and always played on the wing. Coach Hall always said that Harry should concentrate on his own game instead of everyone else's.

Liam was last to go. He adored playing centre forward, but Coach Hall was always complaining that he tried too hard. Liam smiled proudly as he touched the football of *The World's Greatest*, and then lined up next to his team-mates.

"Right, Team!" called Coach Hall. "I want two laps around the pitch, and then we will have a friendly."

As Liam ran alongside Harry, Dominic put his foot out tripping him up. Harry tumbled to the ground and everyone fell about laughing.

"If you can't behave there will be no friendly today!" Coach Hall's voice echoed across the field.

Liam grabbed Harry's arm and whispered in his ear until Harry's eyes opened wide. They ran to the touchline where, standing together, they closed their eyes, took deep breaths and shouted,

"THE POWER OF A TIGER!

THE STRENGTH OF A BEAR!

TAKE THAT BREATH,
AND FLY THROUGH THE AIR!"

Liam looked to Harry. "We are going to be the greatest team in the league!"

"Liam, come on!" Dad's voice squawked. "Stop messing around and get into position!"

Liam felt different. He had loads of energy and he was looking forward to the game.

The whistle blew. Yusef fired the ball down the pitch.

Chin controlled the ball, and passed it to Harry, who ran like lightning down the left wing.

Liam watched carefully, and made sure he was just the right side of the defender. He looked at Harry, who was just getting to the by-line; the ball would be coming to him any second now.

He set off just as Harry made a perfect scooping cross, which Liam lifted his foot to and lobbed the ball into the back of the net.

Everyone cheered – everyone except Liam's dad who just gave him an approving nod. Liam wondered why his Dad never smiled like other dads when he'd scored a goal. All his dad ever did was nod.

The next thing Liam felt was Harry's hand tapping him on the shoulder, at the re-start, as they shared a secret grin.

The ball was off again. Dominic passed to Yusef, Yusef back to Dominic – the perfect one-two. Dominic crossed to Chin.

Harry was ready, he was in position; he had lined himself up perfectly, but he could see Chin was about to lose the ball. Sure enough, there was a battle of boots, and Chin lost the ball in the tackle. Harry could see how Chin could get the ball back, but only if he rushed less and slowed down a little.

The ball was loose on the pitch; but Dominic intercepted it, and crossed it back to Chin who found Harry with an excellent pass.

"Two minutes left, boys!" Coach Hall shouted, pointing to his watch.

Harry belted down the left wing as fast as he could – faster than a cheetah! He dodged one tackle, then turned his foot on the ball, back, forth and around, until he was past the last defender – there was no chance of anyone stopping him now.

Liam ran as fast as he could, and got ready for Harry's pass. They had made a pact, before the game, that they would be strong together – they had power, and they had strength.

Liam pushed with everything that he had. Harry glanced to him, giving him a nod. Liam could see the goal. He could see Harry, and he could see the ball as it left Harry's boot and raced toward him. Instinctively, Liam dived forwards and flew like an eagle, his head connecting with the ball and sending it zooming through the air.

For a moment, there was a silence on the pitch – a silence that was deafening. Liam's heart thumped as the ball skimmed the underside of the bar... and then... dropped perfectly over the line. Harry ran to Liam and climbed on his back shouting, "Power of a tiger! Strength of a bear!" Liam laughed. For a moment, he had forgotten about his dad – something that he had never done before as he always looked for him after scoring a goal. He looked up; his dad nodded as usual, but this time he had a grin on his face – a grin that Liam had never seen till now.

Soon all his team-mates surrounded him and patted him on the back. Liam had netted two in a game before, but he had never scored two amazing goals like today.

Liam knew today was one of the best days he had ever had playing football. Actually, it was one of the best days of his life. Liam was dying to share *The World's Greatest*'s teachings with his team-mates; and he couldn't wait to embark on a new adventure with *The World's Greatest*. He knew deep down inside, in that little place in his tummy, that if his team could get to the final, then one day, maybe, his dream of holding the World Cup at Wembley could come true.

Today, the Mighty Minds team were on their way to being the greatest.

[The End… of The Beginning…]

Can you spot the first letter of the secret word hidden in the Mighty Minds book?

It is a capital letter and it is a different color.

Can you find it?

If you are SUPER CLEVER and you manage to find it then write it on the Mighty Minds ball below.

SUPER CONGRATULATIONS! You are SUPER DOOPER SMART! You have found the first letter of six that make up the Mighty Minds secret word.

Make sure you look out for letter number two in the next Mighty Minds book.

STAY STRONG! STAY HAPPY!

THE WORLDS GREATEST.